GRAPHIC MYTHICAL CREATURES

DRAGONS

BY GARY JEFFREY

ILLUSTRATED BY DHEERAJ VE...

Gareth Stevens
Publishing

Please visit our website, www.garethstevens.com.
For a free color catalog of all our high-quality books,
call toll free 1-800-542-2595 or fax 1-877-542-2596.

Library of Congress Cataloging-in-Publication Data

Jeffrey, Gary.
Dragons / Gary Jeffrey.
p. cm. — (Graphic mythical creatures)
Includes index.
ISBN 978-1-4339-6032-1 (pbk.)
ISBN 978-1-4339-6033-8 (6-pack)
ISBN 978-1-4339-6031-4 (library binding)
1. Dragons—Juvenile literature.. I. Title.
GR830.D7J44 2011
398.24'54—dc22

2010048671

First Edition

Published in 2012 by
Gareth Stevens Publishing
111 East 14th Street, Suite 349
New York, NY 10003

Copyright © 2012 David West Books

Designed by David West Books
Editor: Ronne Randall

Printed in the United States

CPSIA compliance information: Batch #DS11GS: For further information contact Gareth Stevens, New York, New York at 1-800-542-2595.

CONTENTS

Dragons attacking elephants in Roman times

Dragons have been around since ancient times. The ancient Roman naturalist Pliny wrote that *"dragons crave elephant blood in the summer"* and that *"Ethiopian dragons migrate to Arabia once a year to find food."*

EASTERN DRAGONS

In the East, dragons are symbols of good luck or health and are sometimes worshipped. In some places, they are believed to be mythical rulers of weather, especially rain and water. They don't have wings, but use magic to make them fly.

An Eastern dragon

4

A Western dragon

St. George and the Dragon

WESTERN DRAGONS

Dragons in the West have always been regarded as evil and dangerous. They are often depicted guarding treasure and rampaging around the countryside eating humans and livestock. They typically have six limbs, two of which are wings. Often they breathe out vast plumes of fire.

DRAGON SLAYERS

Dragon mythology has often gone hand in hand with the hero dragon slayer. From Hercules of ancient Greek myth to St. George of medieval legend, good is seen battling with evil.

5

BEOWULF AND THE DRAGON

KING BEOWULF OF GOTHLAND SAT ON HIS CHAIR AND LOOKED AT THE CAVE.

I FEEL VERY DISTURBED THAT WE HAVE BEEN FORCED TO COME TO THIS PLACE.

IT WAS RINGED BY STREAMS OF FIRE. EVEN AT THIS DISTANCE, THE MEN COULD FEEL THE HEAT THAT CAME FROM WITHIN.

I REALLY THOUGHT I HAD *FINISHED* WITH ALL OF THIS.

AN OLD WARRIOR AND A LIVING LEGEND, BEOWULF HAD RULED GOTHLAND PEACEFULLY FOR TWENTY YEARS.

IN HIS HAND, HE HELD THE REASON FOR THEIR JOURNEY...

THE CRAFTSMANSHIP IS EXCELLENT — THIS GOBLET REALLY IS A *BEAUTIFUL TROPHY.*

THE OTHERS WATCHED AS BEOWULF STRUGGLED.

HURRRRRR!

HE'S LOSING, AND *BADLY*. AREN'T YOU WARRIORS GOING TO HELP HIM?

ARE YOU JOKING, WIGLAF? AGAINST A *DRAGON*?

WIGLAF WAS ONLY A SERVANT.

IF YOU WON'T

THEN I WILL.

SCRUNCH

GET BEHIND MY **METAL** SHIELD, BOY!

THE OLD KING SUMMONED ALL HIS STRENGTH.

IN HIS YOUTH, BEOWULF HAD SLAIN FLESH-EATING MONSTERS AND SERPENTS...

IT'S TIME TO **END** THIS.

GROOOUGH!

URRRGH – MUST...GET ...MY...KNIFE...

GRAAAAGH!

WHILE THE DRAGON SNAPPED WEAKLY AT WIGLAF, BEOWULF PLUNGED IN HIS KNIFE.

HNNNNGH!

18

...I'M DYING.

THERE WAS NOTHING WIGLAF COULD DO. AS A LAST REQUEST, BEOWULF ASKED TO BE HELPED TO THE DRAGON'S LAIR.

I WANT TO SEE THIS TREASURE I'M **DYING** FOR.

SO MANY CUPS, BRACELETS, AND COLLARS! I HAVE NEVER SEEN SUCH RICHES!

WITH EFFORT, BEOWULF REMOVED HIS OWN GOLDEN COLLAR AND CALLED WIGLAF TO HIM.

THE END

The source for Beowulf and the dragon is an old Anglo-Saxon poem, but dragons feature in myths and legends from all over the world. Here are some of the more well-known dragon tales.

St. George and the Dragon
The story of how the traveling English saint rescues a princess who had been offered to a dragon as a sacrifice.

Maud and the Wyvern
This medieval story tells of a young girl who finds a baby wyvern (a four-limbed dragon) and keeps it as a secret pet, with terrible results.

Kiyohime and the Tale of Dojoji
A story from Japanese folklore in which a waitress, Kiyohime, learns how to turn herself into a flying dragon to punish a man who rejected her.

Rostam and Rakhsh
An ancient Persian hero named Rostam is saved by his horse, Rakhsh, when an invisible dragon creeps up on him while he is sleeping.

Sigurd and Fafnir
An ancient Norse story involving trickery, dragons' blood, and magical changes.

Sigurd kills the dragon Fafnir in its lair.

crave To feel a powerful want for something.

hoard A collection of valuable objects that are carefully guarded.

livestock Valuable farm animals.

lunge To make a sudden forward movement to strike at something.

migrate To move regularly from one region to another, depending on the season.

naturalist An expert in natural history.

plumes Long clouds of smoke or fire that look like feathers as they spread out.

rampaging Rushing around being violent and out of control.

serpent A dragon or mythical, snake-like reptile.

summoned Called forth.

terrorizing Putting a horrible feeling of fear into people.

trophy A hard-won prize.

vast Huge and sweeping.

INDEX